I AM ALL that GOD SAYS I AM

Kingdom Kid Affirmations

Jennifer L. Sargent

Illustration by Ananta Mohanta

Jennifer L. Sargent

Author . Speaker . Entrepreneur

🌐 kingdomkidaffirmations.com

✉️ kingdomkidsaffirmations@gmail.com

f Jennifer L. Sargent

👥 Kingdom Kid Affirmations

📷 _thecrownedjewel_

Affirmation and Book Coach

This book is dedicated to all the wonderful children I have
grown to love and care for at Jennifer's Joyful Journeys.
Remembering our affirmations - always be a good listener, friend, and helper.
Always aim for the stars and dream big! You can do and be anything!
May these words and the love of God forever be planted in your sweet little hearts!
Love, Ms. Jennifer

God is my heavenly Father and He lives in heaven.
All good things come from God, including me!
His holy spirit lives in me, which means
I am beautifully and wonderfully made.
I am all that God says I am!

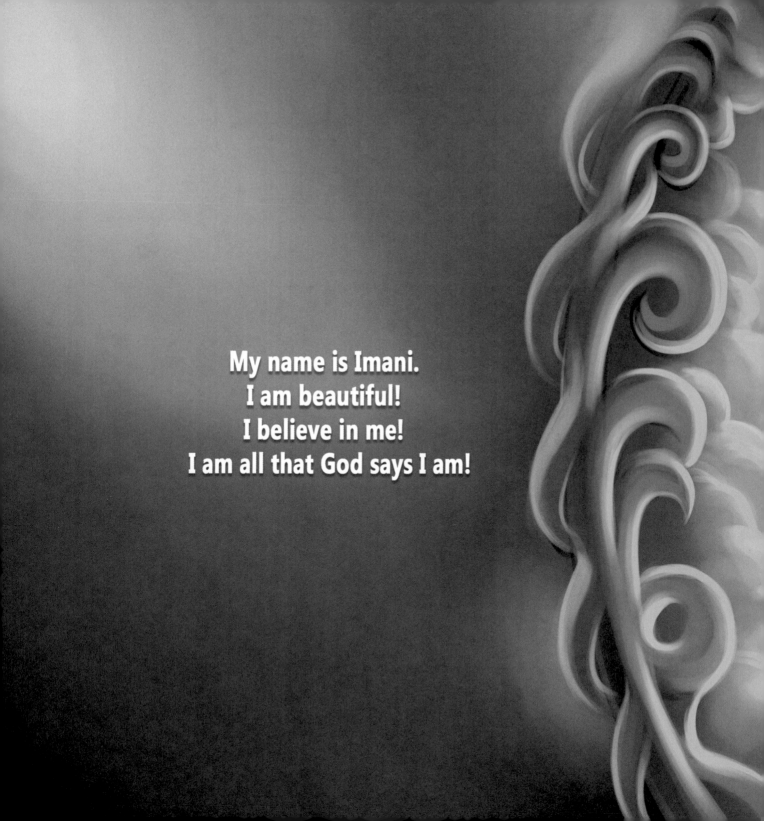

My name is Imani.
I am beautiful!
I believe in me!
I am all that God says I am!

My name is AJ.
I am fun and adventurous!
I believe in me!
I am all that God says I am!

My name is Walter.
I am bold, courageous, and strong!
I believe in me!
I am all that God says I am!

My name is Sophia.
I am kind and friendly!
I believe in me!
I am all that God says I am!

My name is Remy.
am creative and unique!
I believe in me!
am all that God says I am!

My name is Daniel.
I am safe and protected!
I believe in me!
I am all that God says I am!

We are special and we are blessed!
We love who we are and we are changing the world!
We are kingdom kids!
We believe in us!
We are all that God says we are!

To parents and teachers, remember that words are powerful and they change lives!
The power is in our tongues.
Speak life into your kids daily and help them be great!